To Mama, Baba, Annie, Lee, Mimi,
and Niko, with all my heart —CF

To my mom and dad, who continue
to kindly tolerate my messiness —JK

About This Book

The illustrations for this book were done in watercolor and colored pencil on Arches cold-press watercolor paper, and then altered digitally. This book was edited by Nikki Garcia and designed by Véronique Lefèvre Sweet. The production was supervised by Patricia Alvarado, and the production editor was Marisa Finkelstein. The text was set in Garth Graphic Standard, the title was hand-lettered by the artist, and the display type is set in Handy Sans Regular.

Little Messy Marcy Su

Written by **Cherie Fu**

Illustrated by **Julie Kwon**

(L)(B)

Little, Brown and Company

New York Boston

Marcy Su couldn't help but make messes,
track mud on the floors, and get stains on her dresses.
She always had bruises and scrapes on her knees
from running fast races and climbing tall trees.

Early one Sunday, on a bug-hunting scout,
Marcy jumped up when she heard her mom shout—
"Messy Marcy, your room is a sty!
Why can't you clean? Oh, why, Marcy, WHY?

"**Wàipó** and **Wàigōng** are coming today.
Just look at this mess! What will they say?
They'll think you were raised by wolves in the wild.
Or worse, that you're spoiled—an ill-behaved child.

"You ask why I call you my **Xiǎoluànluàn**?
It could be the dirt that's caked onto your hands.
Get yourself dressed, no mud stains allowed.
Please pick up your things, and make Mama proud."

Well, Marcy Su never did shrink from a task.
She thought, "I'll do *more* than my mama had asked.
I'll start out by running the washing machine.
Mama will say, 'Your clothes! **Hǎo gānjìng!**'"

So Marcy ripped out all the family's attire
and polka-dot sheets from the washer and dryer.
The hallway looked like the machines had exploded,
but Marcy was déyì, her own clothes now loaded.

Next, Marcy merrily skipped down the hall
to grab Mama's vacuum plugged into the wall.
She fluttered about, getting fuzz off the floor,
unaware of the chaos raging outside her door—

The twice-tangled cord knocked over the lamp.
Down went the **huāpíng** with Mama's new plant!
The framed family portrait plunged straight to the ground
with a deafening *BANG* and a shattering sound!

Clueless to all the mayhem she'd wrought,
"I need a quick bath!" was Marcy's next thought.
She filled up the tub for a warm, soapy scrub.
She splished and she splashed, singing "Rub-a-dub-dub."

Speeding to dress herself, Marcy was beaming.
Her ribbons pulled tight. But the faucet? Still streaming!
The bubbles were flowing, spilling onto the floor,
soaking the mat as they crept toward the door.

Just then, the **zàoyīn** prompted Mama to check...

and she gasped when she saw that
HER HOME WAS A WRECK!
Who was to blame? Oh, Mama knew who—

"MARCY SU! MARCY SU!
WHAT ON EARTH DID YOU DO?!"

"I stacked all my books—
I can reach the top shelf!

"Did you notice I washed
all my laundry myself?

"I picked up my toys,
so no one will fall.

"I vacuumed the rug.
There are no crumbs at all!

"Don't I look nice? I got myself dressed.
Don't say it. I know. You are truly impressed!"

Mama Su stared, speechless with shock,
unsure what to do as she glanced at the clock.

Just at that moment, the front doorbell chimed,
as **Wàipó** and **Wàigōng** arrived right on time.
Wàipó exclaimed, "**Dàole**! Hello!
The house is a mess! **Āiyā**! Oh no!

"Marcy **bǎobèi**, your room is pristine.
You must have worked the whole morning to clean!

"But the rest of the house—it looks like a zoo!
Why can't the others be more like you?"

Name: **Marcy Su**

Notes from My Chinese Class

What Is Pinyin?

Pinyin uses the Roman alphabet (the same twenty-six letters used for English) to spell out the sound of Mandarin Chinese words. Remember to use the right tone when saying a word, or it will have a different meaning. The symbols above the letters show what tones to use:

- ¯ **first tone**: high, level tone, like the way you'd say "ah" when the doctor checks your throat.

- ´ **second tone**: rising tone, like the way you'd ask "Yes?" when someone calls your name.

- ˇ **third tone**: falling-rising or low tone, like the way you say the second "yo" in "yo-yo."

- ` **fourth tone**: strong falling tone, like the way you'd say "No!" when you're told to eat something you hate!

- **fifth tone (no mark)**: neutral tone.

Words to Practice

Wàipó: maternal grandmother
  sounds like "why-pwo"

Wàigōng: maternal grandfather
  sounds like "why-gong," where the o is long, so the "on" in "gong" sounds like the word "own"

Xiǎoluànluàn: little messy messy
  sounds like "shiao-lwan-lwan," and "shiao" almost rhymes with "cow"

Hǎo gānjìng: so clean
  sounds like "hao-gan-jing," and "hao" almost rhymes with "cow"

Déyì: pleased with oneself
  sounds like "duh-yee"

Huāpíng: flower vase
  sounds like "hwa-ping"

Zàoyīn: noise
  sounds like "zao-yeen," and "zao" almost rhymes with "cow"

Dàole: arrived, like *Made it!* in this context
  sounds like "dao-luh," and "dao" almost rhymes with "cow"

Āiyā: an expression of shock, like *Oh my goodness*
  sounds like "i-ya"

Bǎobèi: darling
  sounds like "bao-bay," and "bao" almost rhymes with "cow"